Edited by
Pauliina Malinen

Designed by
Strawberrie Donnelly

First published in 2018 by Scholastic Children's Books
Euston House, 24 Eversholt Street
London NW1 1DB
a division of Scholastic Ltd
www.scholastic.co.uk
London - New York - Toronto - Sydney - Auckland
Mexico City - New Delhi - Hong Kong

Text and Illustrations copyright © 2018 Sarah McIntyre

HB ISBN 978 1407 14329 3
PB ISBN 978 1407 14330 9

All rights reserved

Printed in Malaysia

1 3 5 7 9 10 8 6 4 2

The moral rights of Sarah McIntyre have been asserted.
Papers used by Scholastic Children's Books are
made from wood grown in sustainable forests.

FOR PHILIP REEVE —
THANKS FOR ALL YOUR
HELP AND SUPPORT
ALONG THE WAY!

DIPSY

FABULOUS FIREFIGHTERS MONTHLY

Dipsy had wanted to be a firefighter since she was a baby Diplodocus, newly hatched from her egg.

Now she was all grown up and she knew IT WAS TIME. She made her way to the Dinoville fire station.

HAVE YOU GOT WHAT IT TAKES?

The chief asked her lots of questions
to see if she might make a good firefighter.
Dipsy's heart went THUMPETY THUMP.
Would she... could she... get this job?

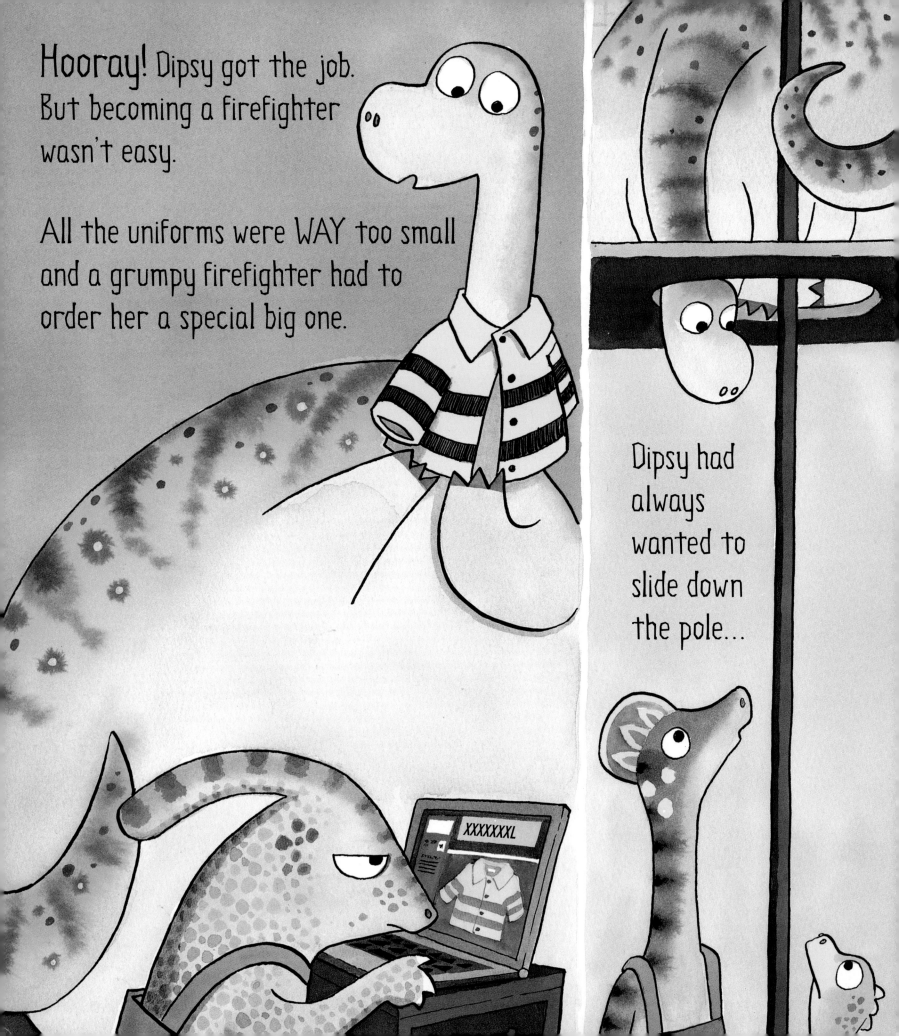

Hooray! Dipsy got the job. But becoming a firefighter wasn't easy.

All the uniforms were WAY too small and a grumpy firefighter had to order her a special big one.

XXXXXXXL

Dipsy had always wanted to slide down the pole...

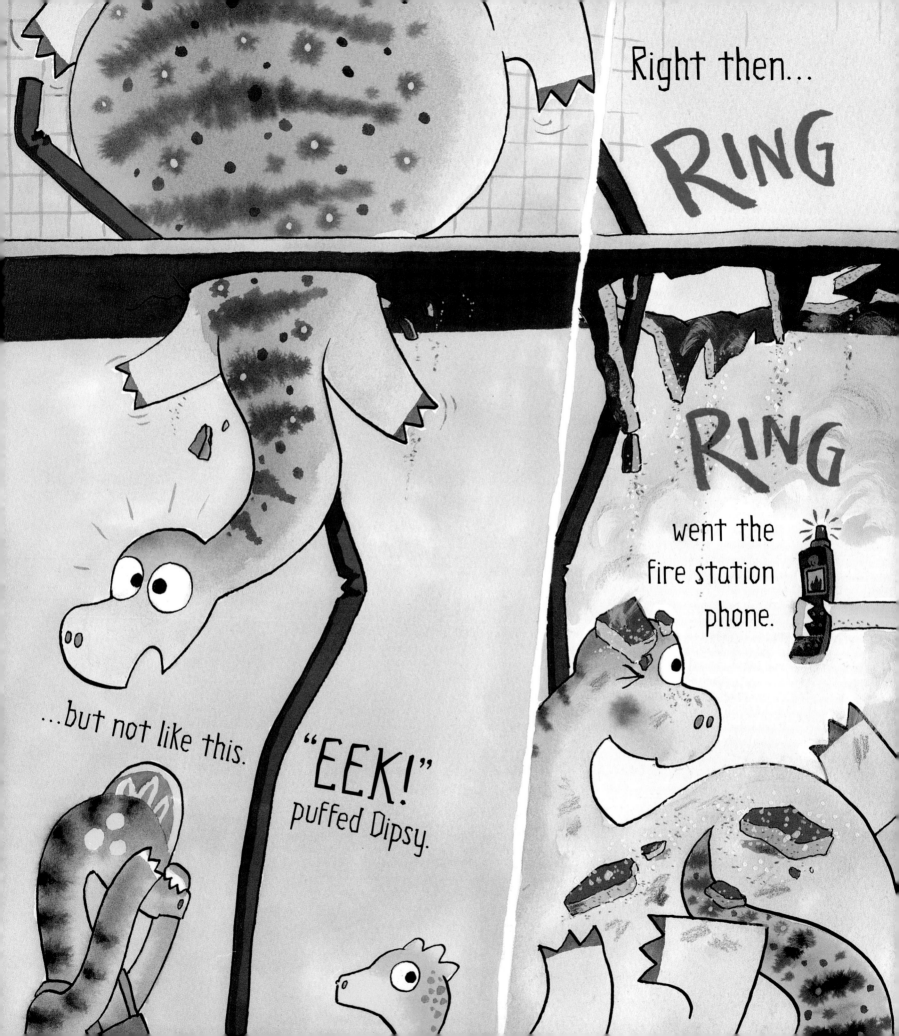

"Please help me!" sobbed Mr Iguanodon. "My little Snookums is stuck in a tree!"

"I can do this!" said Dipsy.

Was this Dipsy's chance to prove herself?

Her long neck was just right for reaching up to the top branch.

But...

Uh-oh! Dipsy pulled that branch too hard and the kitten flew through the air like a fluffy rocket...

... and crash-landed in the mayor's pudding with a...

SPLAT!!

"Whoopsie!" said Dipsy.
"I'm so, so, so sorry!"

NEE-NAR NEE-NAR

Dipsy didn't have much time to worry...they
had another emergency!
"I won't mess things up this time!" she promised.

At the park, Trevor the T-Rex was stuck in the climbing frame.

Firefighter Jamie sighed, "Oh, Trevor, not AGAIN!"

RAWR... RAWR... RAWR!!

Dipsy cut through the metal climbing frame very, very carefully. But she was being SO careful that she didn't notice her tail flicking about...

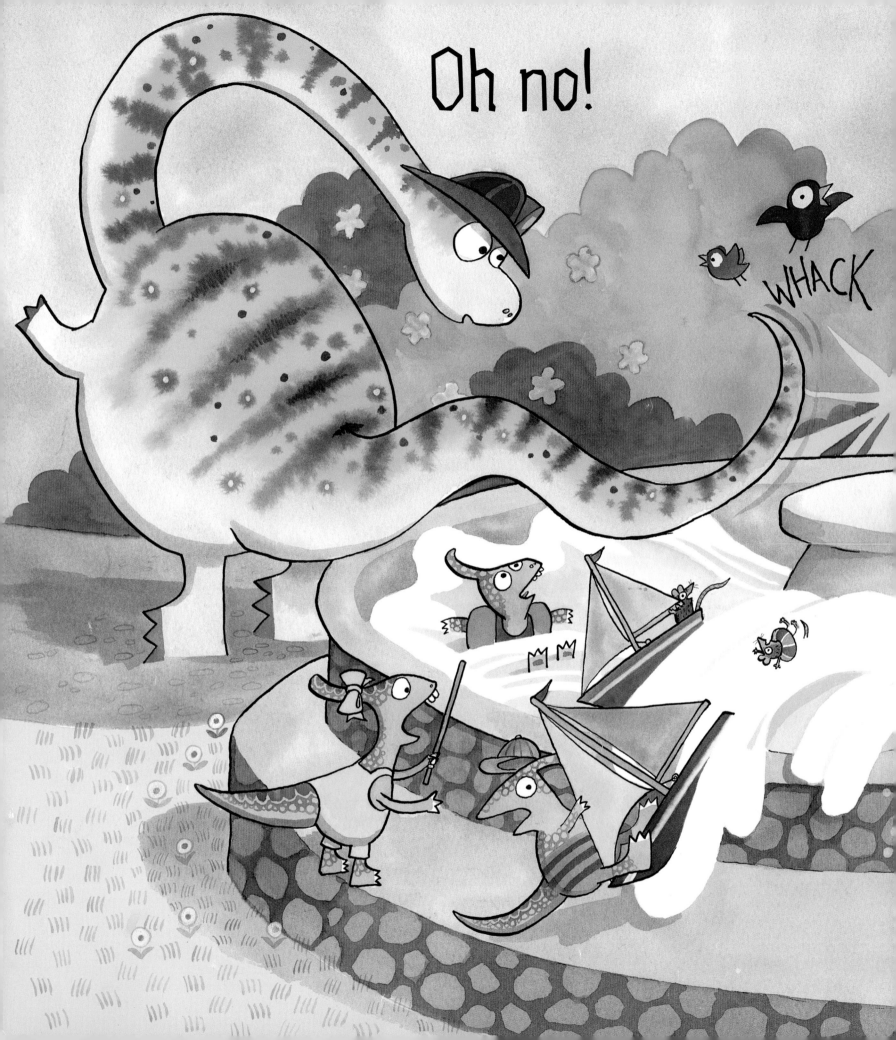

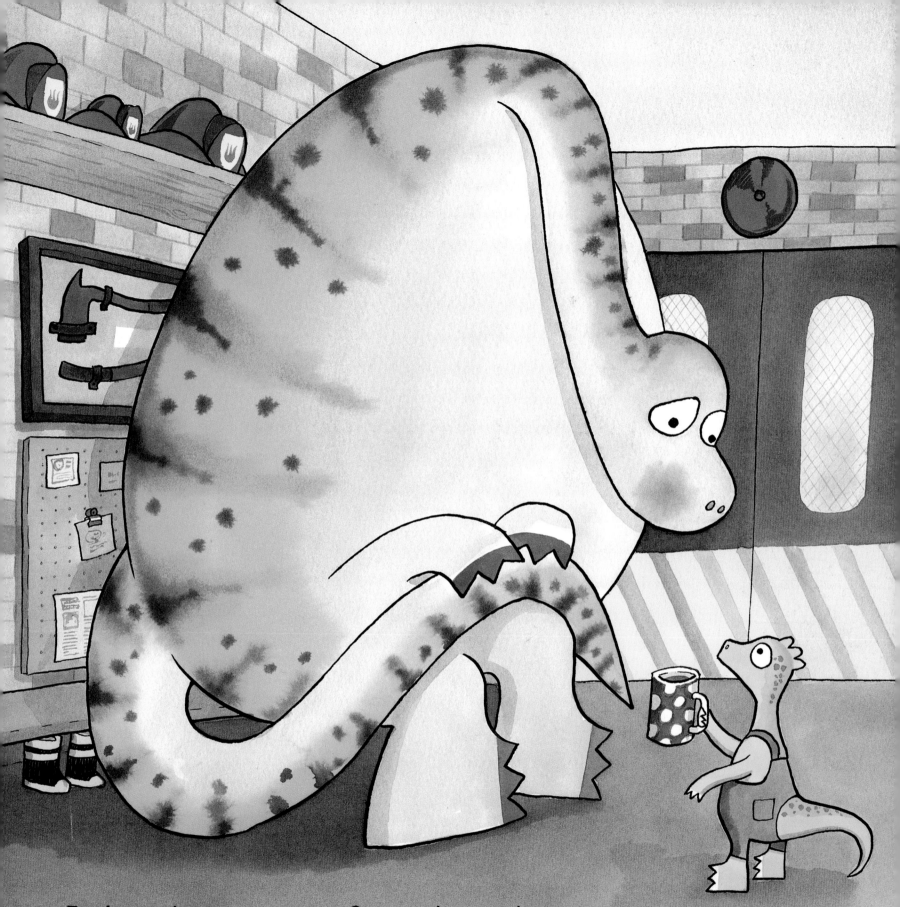

Back at the fire station, Dipsy felt awful.
I'm the worst firefighter EVER, she thought. *I get everything wrong.*

But **leaping lizards!**
The fire engine had broken down. What a **disaster!**

Dipsy had an idea.

"I can be the fire engine!" she roared.
All the firefighters cheered
and jumped on her back.

NEE-
NAR
NEE-
NEE-
NAR!

Dipsy made the siren sound as
they rushed to the rescue.

HELP! shouted the mayor.

THE TOWN HALL IS ON FIRE!

Dipsy stuck out her neck and all the trapped dinosaurs slid down to safety.

Then Dipsy
took a big drink...
and squirted water
onto the burning roof.

YAY!

That fire didn't stand a chance against Dipsy.

The town hall was saved. All the dinosaurs cheered and cheered.

OUR HERO!

The mayor was so happy, she gave Dipsy
a huge shiny medal.
"Hooray for Dipsy, this
town's FINEST fire engine...

...and the BEST firefighter!"

THE END